Richard Scarry's
THINGS TO LEARN

W9-ARP-826

Random House 🏠 New York

GETTING READY
FOR SCHOOL

blanket

"It is time to get up for school,"
said Huckle's mother.
"Why do I have to go to school?"
asked Huckle.
"All children go to school to
learn how to read and write."

Huckle got up.
He yawned and rubbed
the sleep out of
his eyes.

He washed his face with
soap and warm water.

mirror

sink

towel

soap

He brushed his teeth.

pajamas

toothpaste

He combed his hair with cold water.

comb

Then Huckle got dressed.

That is NOT the way to put on your trousers, Huckle!

cap

suspenders

shirt

suit jacket

underpants

sneakers

shoes

socks

Mother Cat gave hot cereal to Huckle
for his breakfast.

bowl

teapot

cup

saucer

brief case

tablecloth

Lowly Worm called in on his way to school. "Hurry,

Mother Cat walked with Huckle
to the school-bus stop.
Honk! Honk!
The school-bus came
to take the children
to school.

or you will be late for school," he said.

This is Huckle's classroom.
Behind the big desk sits Miss Honey,
his teacher.

bell

teacher

paper clips

eraser

ruler

pencil box

workbook

pencil

marker pen

ball-point pen

calendar

SEPTEMBER

SUN	MON	TUES	WED	THU	FRI	SAT
			1	2	3	4	5
6	7	8	9	10	11	12
13	14	15	16	17	18	19
20	21	22	23	24	25	26
27	28	29	30			

$$2+1=3$$
$$2+2$$

pencil sharpener

paste pot

blackboard
eraser

scissors

chalk

Richard Scarry's
What Do
People Do
All Day?

storybook

thumbtacks

Each day Miss Honey
teaches her class
something new.

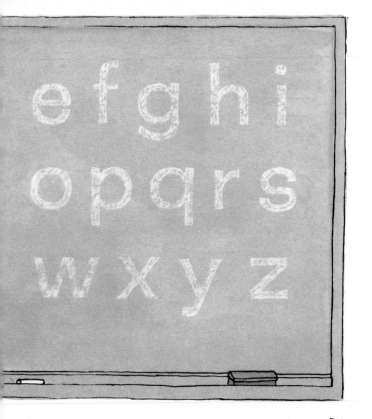

Today she is going to teach them the alphabet.
Do YOU know the alphabet?
It's a good thing to learn.

LEARNING NUMBERS

Do you know how to count?
I'll bet you do!
Can you count how many
pirates there are?

7

8

9

10

THE PLAYGROUND

Everybody is doing something.

What do you think is the most fun?

rings

sliding pole

stilts

pat-a-cake

shovel

pail

sandbox

swing

tag

jump rope

leapfrog

hopscotch

7 8 6 4 5 3 2 1

SPRING

wash

There is a sweet smell in the air.

Flower seeds float on the breeze.

narcissus

tulip

violet

crocus

Lowly Worm

kite

airplane

Farmer Fox plows
his field for
spring planting.

plow

lily of
the valley

tractor

daffodil

dandelion

GASOLINE

gas pump

gas storage tank

GARDENER

OIL

AT THE FILLING STATION

At the busy, busy filling station, all kinds of
trucks come in to get oil and gas. The
attendants haven't even had time to cover up
the new underground storage tank.
What do you think the carpenter is going to
build with all that wood?

MACHINES

Machines help people to do their work.

cotton picker

wheat field

Eli Cottontail picks cotton balls with his cotton picker.

power shovel

Big heavy rocks are loaded into the rock crusher.

combine harvester

chaff

wheat grain

Farmer Pig gathers his crop
with a harvesting machine.

rock crusher

These road builders use many
different machines to build
a road.

The grader makes
the ground smooth

ditch digger

Digger Dog is digging a ditch
for the big water pipe.

The bulldozer
moves earth

The motor crane
lifts heavy things

SUMMER

In the summertime, it is fun to go and play
on the beach.

beach
umbrella

shovel

sand
castle

pail

paper plates

sea shell

ball

crab

waves

a diving pig

lobster

AT THE AIRPORT

Father Cat took Huckle and Little Sister to the airport. Rudolf, the famous pilot, showed them how a plane works.

tail

rudder

elevator

fuselage

aileron

wing

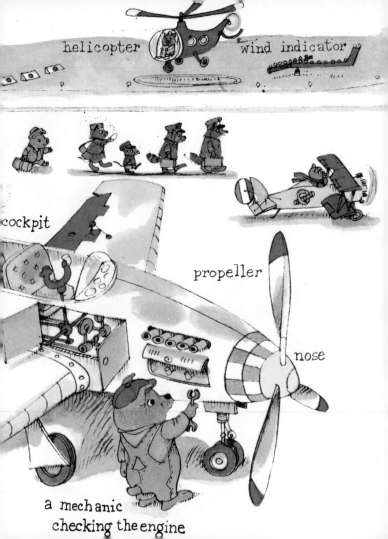

helicopter

wind indicator

cockpit

propeller

nose

a mechanic
checking the engine

THE AIR SHOW

All these pilots are flying famous
old military airplanes—except one.
Can you find him?

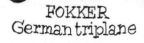

FOKKER
German triplane

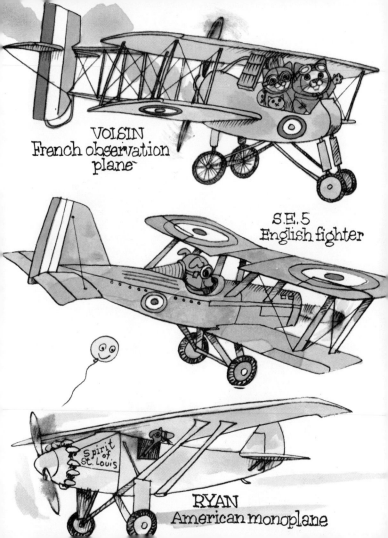

VOISIN
French observation
plane

S.E.5
English fighter

Spirit
of
St. Louis

RYAN
American monoplane

trumpet

THE MUSICIANS

Miss Honey is practicing with
the class orchestra. She plays
the bass fiddle. What musical
instrument would you like to
learn to play?

violin

bass
drum

flute

piano

clarinet

accordion

bassoon

saxophone

cymbals

bass
fiddle

guitar

harp

THE HARBOR

Here is a busy harbor full of boats. Who likes to sail in a glass boat?

Lowly Worm!

quay

motorboat

racer

lifeboat

bridge

bow

portholes

tug

rowboat

speedboat

bottle

HELP!

gangplank

pier

signal
flag

rope

police launch

submarine

Lowly
Worm

THE FALL

windmill

The leaves turn red and brown and fall off the trees. Soon winter will be here.

miller

hat

grain

HUCKLE

rake

chimney

haystack

cottage

Farmer Fox

apple tree

leaves

ladder

OPPOSITES

There are many different kinds of shapes and sizes. *Little* is the opposite of *big*. *Thin* is the opposite of *fat*. Can you find other "opposites"?

little

big

fat

thin

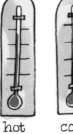

hot   cold

round

square

long

short

straight

curved

crooked

pull

push

young

old

COLORS

fire engine

heart

apple

strawberry

the inside of
a watermelon

Drawing and painting are always fun.
Can you name all the colors? Try.

Arthur Pig paints a
red apple on the paper.

paint   water

ORANGE

Daddy Pig paints his boat orange.

orange

goldfish

pumpkin

carrot

bus

YELLOW

Yellow is a bright,
sunny color.
Can you name all the
things that are
yellow?

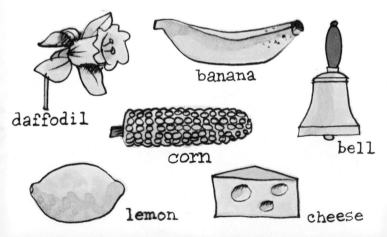

daffodil

banana

corn

bell

lemon

cheese

peas

leaf

blades of grass

lettuce

pine tree

clover leaf

GREEN

Many things that grow are green.
Huckle painted the car green. Now he
has green paint all over himself.

BLUE

easel

Big Hilda's favorite color is blue. What color do you think she is going to paint her drawing? What color would YOU paint it?

sailboat

blueberries

bluebells

PURPLE

Purple is almost the same color as violet.

violet

plum

pansy

thistle

grape

BROWN

 walnut

potato

shoelace

chocolate
Easter Bunny

Colors can be light or dark.
A potato is light brown.
A chocolate Easter bunny
is dark brown.
Huckle mixes red and black to get
brown paint.

red   black

BLACK

doorbell

licorice gumdrop

hat

tire

black

white

Black is the opposite of white.

egg

snowman

WINTER

It is fun to play in the snow or on the ice. Did you ever try to build a snowman?

ski pole

skis

sled

snowshoes

snowball fight

snow fort

scarf

SCHOOL BUS

broom

snowman

hockey stick

puck

ice skater

AT THE HEALTH CLINIC

From time to time, children must visit the doctor
to make sure they are well and healthy. They also
find out how tall they have grown...

height measure

scales

...and how much they weigh.

Say AHHHH.

bandage

Band-Aid

forceps

thermometer

flashlight

tongue
stick

adhesive tape